Bertie and the
ALIEN
CHICKEN

JENNY PEARSON

Illustrated by
Aleksei Bitskoff

Barrington Stoke

To Oliver "Brian" West

First published in 2023 in Great Britain by
Barrington Stoke Ltd
18 Walker Street, Edinburgh, EH3 7LP

www.barringtonstoke.co.uk

Text © 2023 Jenny Pearson
Illustrations © 2023 Aleksei Bitskoff

A CIP catalogue record for this book is available
from the British Library upon request

ISBN: 978-1-80090-181-0

Printed by Hussar Books, Poland

CONTENTS

CHAPTER 1

What do you find on a farm?

Ask anyone what they would find on a farm, and they would probably say something like, "Cows, pigs, sheep."

Not, "An alien chicken with a bit of an attitude problem."

But that's exactly what I found when I went to stay at Long Bottom Farm with my Uncle Brian this summer.

To be honest, I was not thrilled about the idea of staying with my uncle. I'd been for a few day visits over the years, but I'd never stayed over. Farms aren't really my thing. I might have been more pumped about my visit if I'd known about the adventure I'd have with Nugget, the alien chicken, saving the world. But as it was, I didn't. So I was very *not* pumped.

We were in the car on the way to the farm when I presented Mum with a list of reasons why I should go with her on her work trip to America instead.

"Mother," I said, in my most businessy voice, "I would like to discuss this small matter of me going to stay with Uncle Brian. This is NOT going to be an awesome summer holiday!"

"You're going," Mum said. "Discussion over."

I wasn't going to be beaten that fast. "I shall start with point one," I went on. "The place stinks!"

"It's a farm – it's a good smell," Mum said.

"A good smell?" I said. "Are you kidding? It smells so bad that you have to breathe using your mouth. Even then, I'm sure the smell seeps into your eyeballs and earholes."

"Don't be over-dramatic," Mum told me.

"On to point two," I added. "The farm is in the countryside."

"Yes, Bertie," Mum said, giving a big sigh. "That's where they tend to be."

"The countryside is not exactly the entertainment centre of the UK," I pointed out. "There's no skate park, no arcade, no shopping centre and none of my mates are in the countryside! I'll be lonely."

I said *lonely* very sadly in the hope that Mum might feel a bit sorry for me.

But nope.

"It will do you good," Mum said. "Besides, you'll have lots of animals to spend time with."

"You want me to make friends with the livestock?"

"Why not?" Mum asked.

"Why not? *Why not?*" I replied.

"You're going to have a fantastic time."

"Oh yeah, me and the cows will be best buddies. Point three!" I continued. "Uncle Brian's a bit ... weird."

Mum tilted her head. "I wouldn't say weird," she said.

"Mum, he drank milk that he had just squeezed from a cow's udder into a bucket last time I was there!" I shuddered. "Cow. Udder. Squeeze-squeeze. Bucket. Mouth. Gone! Just like that!"

"That's where milk comes from, Bertie," Mum said, like it was perfectly normal to use a cow like a drinking fountain.

"Do you think all the gas from the animal farts has messed up his brain?" I asked.

"Don't be ridiculous," Mum snapped. "Look, your uncle Brian doesn't have kids of his own, and he's delighted to have you to stay. I'm sure he'll enjoy the company. Now, is that it?"

"No, that's not it!" I replied. "I have another point. Number four – the place smells soooo bad."

"You already said that."

"Yeah, but it's so bad, I think it needs to be mentioned twice."

"You'll get used to it."

"And I definitely can't go to Dad's?" I said quietly.

Mum's face softened. "Oh, sweetheart, you know Dad would have you to visit if he could."

"Why can't he?" I asked. "A new baby can't need that much looking after."

My dad had just had a baby with his girlfriend, Nancy. I was trying to be happy for them. But I wasn't. Not really. Dad had already left me. Now he'd replaced me too.

"You can visit him soon, I promise," Mum said. "You're going to have the best time with Uncle Brian, pumpkin."

"I'm not a pumpkin, and I'm not going to have the best time," I said, and slunk down in my seat. "I'm going to be soooo bored."

But it turned out I was completely wrong about the being bored thing.

Hanging around with an alien chicken called Nugget was not boring in the slightest.

CHAPTER 2

What are you doing yelping at a chicken?

The drive to Long Bottom Farm was both long and terrifying. It was long because Mum kept getting lost down all the tiny roads that led to the farm. It was terrifying because Mum was worried about missing her flight. This meant she drove like an angry racing-car driver. Even Lewis Hamilton would have found it hard to beat her.

Our car screeched up to Uncle Brian's door. He was in the yard, in front of the farmhouse. He gave us a nod. Uncle Brian couldn't wave because he was pushing a wheelbarrow.

Long Bottom Farm is made up of:

1. the farmhouse where Mum and Uncle Brian grew up

2. a barn full of haybales

3. a chicken shed

4. about ten pig sties

5. a cow shed

6. lots and lots of fields.

I got out of the car, and the smell punched me right in both nostrils.

"Hate to do this, but I have to dash off straight away, Bri!" Mum hollered to my uncle. She leapt out of the car and went to hug Uncle Brian but then stopped and screwed up her nose. I wasn't surprised she changed her mind. Uncle Brian was covered in a lot of brown muck.

Mum then grabbed my bags from the boot and gave me a hug. "Be good, Bertie! Have fun!"

"Mum," I whispered. "It really stinks. I can't stay here. I think my nose will fall off from the smell."

She crossed her arms. "The only thing that stinks around here is your attitude, young man."

"But—" I began.

"No buts," Mum said. "Positive thinking only!" She gave me a big smile and an even bigger kiss. Then she shouted to Uncle Brian, "Look after him!"

And off Mum went, calling out, "America, here I come!"

I was in a proper grump. I'd been deserted by both my parents.

Uncle Brian held out his huge hand for me to shake. "Bertie, good to see you," he said. "Don't you worry. You'll be all right with me."

I looked at Uncle Brian's hand. Then at the wheelbarrow he'd been pushing. It was full of manure.

I know it's polite to shake someone's hand when you meet. But what if they've been shovelling around animal poo? I couldn't bring myself to put my hand in his. So I just kept looking at it. Which got a bit awkward after thirty seconds.

"Not shy, are you?" Uncle Brian laughed. Then he slapped me on the back.

"Nope," I said grumpily because I was deep in my grump.

Uncle Brian nodded towards the house. "Dump your bags inside. Then you can help me move the cows into the back field. The other farm lads are busy mucking out the pigs."

Move cows? I definitely had no cow-moving skills. "How?"

"Ask them nicely."

See, I told you Uncle Brian was weird.

I frowned. "Really? Ask them?" I said.

"You try it and see how it goes." Uncle Brian grinned, and his eyes went all crinkly. "Best you change into some wellies."

I looked down at my best trainers. The ones Dad had sent me last time he cancelled my visit. They were already covered in farm muck, just from the yard. I gave my feet an angry shake to try to get the mud off.

"What are you waiting for?" Uncle Brian said. "Cows won't move themselves."

I stomped off towards the house, not delighted about having to do cow moving. I was grumbling to myself about how completely unfair life is, when a chicken flew into my face

out of nowhere. Well, not exactly into my face, but it was close.

I was so surprised that I screamed.

I know. Screaming at a chicken isn't very brave. I have two points to make in my defence. Point one – I do get braver later in the story. Point two – this was no ordinary chicken.

But I didn't know that the first time I screamed at it. At the time, it looked like a regular chicken. It had all the regular chicken parts. Feathers. Beak. Horrible knobbly feet. Beady little eyes.

After I'd screamed, I heard myself say, "Sorry." You know, like you do when you bump into a shop dummy or a lamp post? The word "sorry" comes out of your mouth before you realise you don't have to say it. A shop dummy or a lamp post isn't going to mind that you've bumped into them.

Well, I didn't think a chicken would mind if I screamed at it. So I felt a bit daft about apologising.

But as it turned out, the chicken *was* a bit miffed about me screaming at it. How did I know? Because the chicken said, "I should think so too!" Then it said, "Whoops!" and covered its beak with its wing, like it shouldn't have said that.

This is when I screamed again.

I know.

Screaming at a chicken twice definitely isn't that brave. But back to point two – this was no ordinary chicken. This was now a *talking* chicken.

After my second scream, the chicken flapped away and Uncle Brian rushed over.

"You all right, Bertie?" Uncle Brian was frowning. "What are you doing yelping at a chicken?"

"Ch ... ch ... chicken!" was all I managed to say.

"You're not scared of chickens, are you?"

"Ch ... ch ... chicken ... talked."

"What?" Uncle Brian asked.

"That chicken!" I said, pointing to it with a shaky finger. "That chicken spoke."

Uncle Brian looked over to where the chicken was strutting about the yard. It looked very ... well ... chicken-like.

Uncle Brian rubbed his bristly face with his hand. "Are you feeling OK, Bertie?"

"That chicken! It spoke!" I explained. "It said, *I should think so too*."

"That chicken?" Uncle Brian looked at the chicken, which was now clucking and not speaking.

Then he looked back at me.

Then back at the chicken.

Then back at me.

Then Uncle Brian slapped me on the back. Again. And did a big laugh. "You almost had me there, Bertie," he said. "Now hurry up and get changed. I'll meet you over by the gate."

Uncle Brian wandered off down the drive muttering, "Talking chicken! Whatever next?"

I looked at the chicken.

It eyeballed me back. In what I thought was a bit of a threatening way.

"You spoke. I know you did," I whispered.

I don't know what I was expecting, but I wasn't expecting the chicken to hold up its wing to its beak and say, "Shhhhh."

Which is exactly what it did!

"Uncle Brian!" I yelled. "The chicken shushed me!"

Uncle Brian didn't stop. He laughed and yelled back at me, "Yeah, right, and once a cow asked me to a dance!"

I know I sounded ridiculous. Chickens don't talk. I glared at it. Clearly, I was imagining things. Maybe the stinking farm fumes were already affecting my brain.

But the chicken set its evil eyes on me.
Then it ran its wing across its throat and said,
"Silence, Earthling. Or I, the High Emperor of
Nurgle-7, will exterminate you."

That's when I screamed at a chicken for
the third time.

CHAPTER 3

How *exactly* do you move cows?

After the chicken had finished threatening me, it flapped off towards the chicken shed. I watched it go, my mouth open and mind whirling.

That *couldn't* have just happened! There was *no way* it had just happened. It was probably my overactive imagination. I do have an excellent imagination. The stress of being abandoned by both my parents probably wasn't helping either. There was no such thing as a talking chicken. Or Nurgle-7 – whatever *that* was.

I gave myself a shake, then headed into the house. I needed to get changed to help Uncle Brian with the cows.

Mum had packed my all-in-one waterproof outfit. It was a bit small and gave me an instant wedgie. I walked out to the gate on tippy-toes, trying to pull my boxers out from between my bum cheeks. As I went, I kept an eye out for any angry farm birds – just in case.

Uncle Brian frowned when he saw me. "You OK?" he asked.

"Fine," I said. But I really wasn't. I couldn't get that threatening chicken out of my head. Or my underwear out of my bum crack.

Uncle Brian was leaning on the gate, chewing a piece of grass. "Get yourself into the field and start rounding the cows up."

There were about thirty black-and-white cows wandering about. Some of them were chewing grass like Uncle Brian. They didn't look threatening. Not by weird chicken standards. But they did look big.

"You want me to go in there?" I said. "With them?"

Uncle Brian opened the gate. "Yup. Just coax them this way. Then lead them down the track to the other field."

Coax a herd of cows. How do you coax a herd of cows?

Well, not by saying, "Come on, nice cowies," which I tried. Or, "Walkies," which I also tried.

"Show them who's boss," Uncle Brian said at last, after he'd stopped chuckling. "Whoop a bit."

"Whoop?" I said.

"Yeah, whoop."

So I tried whooping.

"Give it a bit more welly," Uncle Brian said.

I whooped a bit louder and ran around waving my arms. The cows didn't move. In fact, they looked completely uninterested.

"It's not working!" I said, and turned to Uncle Brian. He had a big grin plastered across his face.

"Could always try using the feed to get them out. That's what we normally do."

Uncle Brian winked at me.

"You've been messing with me!" I said, feeling a bit daft and a bit angry about my whooping and arm flapping.

"Here, take this," Uncle Brian said, handing me a bucket of feed. But I wasn't in the mood, and I stomped back to the house.

CHAPTER 4

What's a Nurgle?

Uncle Brian came into my room after he had sorted the cows. He was holding this long pole thing with a disc on the end of it.

"Sorry about earlier – just having a little joke," he said.

I grunted because I was still cross with him.

"Look, I've got to go help Perry and Bernard with the pigs," Uncle Brian explained.

Perry and Bernard have worked at Long Bottom Farm for years. I've met them a few times, but I find it hard to tell them apart. They are both the same height. Both a sort of square shape and both have big beards which take up most of their faces.

"Go and help them then," I said grumpily.

"Thought you might like to have a play with this," Uncle Brian said, handing the long pole thing to me.

"What is it?" I asked.

"A metal detector. Thought you could go and hunt for treasure."

A metal detector. I had to admit that sounded cool. I started imagining all the things I would find. Old coins. Ancient gold. Roman weapons!

I did not think for one second that I would discover a tiny spaceship from Nurgle-7.

But who would?

"Thanks," I said. I know you shouldn't like people more because they give you presents, but it did make me warm to Uncle Brian a bit.

*

I let myself feel grumpy at the cow thing and at Mum and Dad a little longer. Then I headed outside to play with the detector.

I went round the back of one of the barns and waved the metal detector over the earth, keeping an eye out for *that* chicken. The detector soon started bleeping. I quickly found a screw, a nail and a bit of scrap metal. It went on like that for an hour. I started to think I'd never find anything exciting.

But then it bleeped again, and the bleeps grew louder. More furious. The detector started to shake hard. It was difficult to hold on to it! Then it blew up! Well, when I say *blew up*, the detector fizzed, crackled and popped, then smoke came out of it.

It was a bit of a surprise, and I reacted by launching the detector across the yard. It landed with a bit of a crash.

My first thought was, *Oh no, I've broken Uncle Brian's metal detector.*

My second thought was, *What on earth did it detect?*

I couldn't do much about my first thought. So I grabbed my spade and started digging. A few centimetres under the earth, I hit something hard. Carefully, I moved the dirt away.

That's when I saw it.

Something shiny and purple. Shaking with excitement, I dug down deeper until I could pull it out.

It was smooth and egg-shaped, about the size of the bucket I'd been using to collect the metal. It felt warm and was buzzing slightly.

"Woah! What is this?" I said out loud.

"That is Voyager 9. My spacecraft."

I wasn't expecting a reply.

I turned around slowly.

There behind me was *that* chicken.

I opened my mouth to scream at the chicken for a fourth time. But I must have used up all my chicken-screams for the day as no sound came out.

"Put it down, or prepare to be exterminated," the chicken said.

I stood there. Not moving. Not screaming. Just totally shocked.

The chicken tilted its head and said, "Put it down, Earthling, or meet your doom."

I still didn't react. I think my brain was having trouble deciding what to do. It's not every day you're threatened by poultry repeatedly.

"I'm not joking," the chicken said. "Put it down. I'm going to count down from three. Three ... two ... one ... one and a half ... one and a quarter ... one and an eighth ..."

It was when the chicken got to one and a 512th that I realised it wasn't going to exterminate me. It was a chicken! How dangerous could it be?

I relaxed a bit.

"You're a chicken," I said. "A talking chicken, but still just a chicken. What exactly do you think you're going to do to me?"

"I'll ... I'll ... peck your eyes out," the chicken said.

To be honest, the chicken didn't sound that certain.

"Go on," I said, calling its bluff. "Peck away."

The chicken hesitated. Then crossed its wings. "Fine. I'm not going to peck your eyes out."

"Ha! I knew it!" I said.

"But I'm not a chicken."

I looked it up and down. "You look like a chicken," I said. "You've got the feathers and everything!"

"I'm a Nurgle."

"A *what?*"

It stretched its wings skywards and said, "I come from the planet Nurgle-7."

"You're an alien?! From outer space?"

"Yes, if you want to call me that, I'm an alien," he replied.

I thought about it. I supposed an alien was as possible as a talking chicken. I held up the purple spacecraft. "And you came here in this egg?"

"That is not an egg!" the alien chicken said. "It's more of a capsule."

"It looks like an egg," I replied.

"It's not an egg! It's a highly complex space voyager."

"I never thought aliens would be chickens," I went on. "I'd always imagined them to be green and a bit slimy."

"I'm not a chicken," he said.

"You *look* like a chicken."

"This," he said, holding out his wings, "was a bit of an accident."

"An accident?" I asked.

"When I landed on Earth, I transformed myself to avoid detection."

"You transformed into a *chicken*? Why?"

"I thought that is what Earthlings looked like," he explained.

"You thought we looked like *chickens*?"

"They were the first life-form I came across when I arrived."

"You thought Earth was inhabited by chickens?" I said. Frankly, the alien chicken didn't sound that smart to me.

"There were an awful lot of chickens in that shed. It made sense at the time." He gave a big sigh, then sat down. "And now I can't change back. My mission is ruined. I am doomed to live out the rest of my days like this."

The alien chicken started crying. Big squawky sobs.

"Don't cry," I said. I know saying *don't cry* never works, but I really had no idea how to comfort an alien chicken.

I had a million questions – about what a Nurgle was and why it was here. But the main thing I was thinking was, *Poor little fella*. I felt so sorry for him. Far away from his home. Stuck on a stinky farm. All alone. Just like me.

I decided there and then that I would help him.

CHAPTER 5

A Nurgle agreement ritual is *what?*

The alien chicken carried on crying. I sat down beside him. "Sorry you're in a spot of trouble," I said. "I'm Bertie."

"Nugglynugglynoonahnoo." He raised his wing, and I gave it a shake.

"Is that your name?" I asked. "Nuggly … nuggly … noo-nah? It's a bit of a mouthful."

"Not for a Nurgle," he sniffed. "But you can call me Nugget for short."

"As in *chicken* nugget?" I said, trying not to laugh.

Nugget didn't look amused. "No, as in Nurgle Nugget. What's a chicken nugget?"

"Best you don't know," I said.

Nugget sobbed some more. "I can't believe I'm stuck here. I'm a failure. A feathery failure!"

"Why did you come here in the first place?" I asked.

"I was sent on a mission to find Earth's most valuable resource."

"What's Earth's most valuable resource?"

"I don't know!" Nugget wailed. "That's the mission, genius. To find Earth's most valuable resource."

I did not like the way Nugget said *genius*, as if he didn't think I was one. Nugget was the one who had turned himself into a chicken, not me!

"What are you going to do with it when you've found it?" I asked.

"Take some of it back to Nurgle-7 to study."

"Why don't you just go back now? I don't think you're going to be able to complete your mission as a chicken."

"If I go back now, I will have failed," Nugget said. "I will be sent to the D-zone."

"What's the D-zone?" I asked.

Nugget shivered. "Let's just say I'd rather spend the rest of my days scratching at the earth and eating worms than be sent there."

"Couldn't you explain to whoever is in charge?" I said. "Hang on ... before, you said you were the High Emperor of Nurgle-7. Aren't *you* in charge?"

Nugget shook his head. "I might have made that up," he said. "Just to sound more threatening. The real High Emperor won't listen to an explanation from me. The rules are the rules."

"So you're stuck here?" I sat for a moment and tried to think of a way to help. But all I could think of was that it would be pretty cool to have a talking chicken as a pet.

"Maybe being here won't be so bad?" I suggested.

Nugget sighed. "It won't be for long anyway."

"What do you mean, it won't be for long?" I asked. An image of a chicken nugget popped into my head.

"If I don't return with Earth's most valuable resource by the end of today, the High Emperor will think there isn't a valuable resource on Earth."

"And then what happens?" I said.

"Earth will be exterminated."

"WHAT?" I shouted. "That's a bit extreme!"

"There's no sense in a planet that doesn't offer anything useful."

"WHAT? Earth is very useful!"

"In what way?" Nugget asked.

"I live on it, for a start!"

"I'm not talking about it being useful for Earthlings. I'm talking about it being useful for Nurgles. You see we have pretty much everything we need on Nurgle-7. Anything I present to them from Earth needs to be pretty special."

"There's loads of things on Earth that are useful!" I said. "I'll show you!"

Nugget cocked his head. "There are?"

"Yes! Earth is a wonderful place. Full of fantastic things."

"Like?" Nugget asked.

"Like … television and chocolate and trees and … and … well, loads of stuff. I will not allow your Nurgle High Emperor to exterminate it. They can't just decide Earth is useless!"

"Are you offering to help me?" Nugget asked.

"You bet I am!"

"This is the greatest news. Now you must join me in the Nurgle agreement ritual."

"The *what*?" I said.

"The Nurgle agreement ritual. It bonds you to our promise."

"OK ..."

"Turn around," Nugget instructed.

I turned around.

"Now bang your backside into mine to seal your promise."

I spun back to face him.

"You want me to *what*?" I asked.

"Bang your backside into mine."

"I'm not doing that!"

"The safety of your planet depends on it," Nugget said.

So that was the day I bumped bums with an alien chicken and became responsible for saving the world.

CHAPTER 6

Why is manure important?

I'd just finished hiding Nugget's spacecraft in a haystack round the back of the barn when Uncle Brian appeared with someone. I guessed this was Perry or Bernard.

"Is that your talking chicken?" Uncle Brian said, clocking Nugget.

"No, it is a regular chicken," I said. "Definitely not a talking chicken. Or an alien."

Uncle Brian gave me a strange look. Which was probably deserved.

Perry or Bernard scrunched up his nose. "Not a fan of chickens myself," he said. "You know they are descended from dinosaurs? Pterodactyls, probably."

"Don't tell Bertie that, Bernard!" Uncle Brian said. "He's already scared of the things!"

"I'm not! It just leapt out of nowhere," I replied.

"Do chickens leap?" Bernard asked.

"This one did," I said.

Uncle Brian nodded at the metal detector and asked, "You find anything interesting?"

"No! Nothing!" I panic-shouted. "Nothing interesting at all. Just bits of scrap metal. But it's a great present. Thank you."

I didn't think I'd be able to explain a Nurgle space voyager craft to them. Uncle Brian was sure to think I was making it up.

He smiled. "Good. I'm pleased. You hungry?"

I wasn't hungry. Knowing I had to save the planet from the Nurgles was affecting my appetite. I hadn't a clue what the most valuable resource was on Earth. I needed to get thinking.

"I think I might just hang out here," I said.

"With the chicken?" Bernard asked, grinning.

"You need to eat, lad," Uncle Brian said. "Come on. Your mum tasked me with looking after you, and that's what I shall do."

I didn't have much choice but to follow Uncle Brian and Bernard. Maybe they might know what Earth's most valuable resource was. It couldn't hurt to ask.

"Here! Would you look at that?" Bernard said as we started walking back to the house. "That chicken is following us."

I glared at Nugget, but he followed me all the way to the house.

"Made a pal there, Bertie," Uncle Brian said when we reached the front door.

Uncle Brian and Bernard went inside, but I stopped to have a word with Nugget.

"What are you doing? You can't come in!" I said.

Nugget cocked his head. "But we are bonded by the Nurgle agreement," he said. "We must stay together at all times."

"I can't be with you at all times!"

"Why not?"

"Because chickens are outdoor animals!" I said.

"But I am not a chicken. I am a Nurgle."

"Yes, but you *look* like a chicken!"

"And you *made* an agreement," Nugget pointed out.

"But you didn't tell me about the being stuck with you at all times part!" I explained.

"You didn't ask."

"Why would I have asked *that*? Look, I can't take you inside. Uncle Brian will ask questions."

Nugget shrugged. "Then you will have to answer them," he said. "There is not long until your world will be destroyed."

And then Nugget strutted past me and wandered off to the kitchen.

"Oi! I said, running after him. "You'd better keep your beak shut!"

In the kitchen, Uncle Brian was already busy making cheese sandwiches. Bernard and Perry were both sitting at the kitchen table, drinking pints of milk and looking exactly like each other.

I took off my waterproof all-in-one and sat down at the table, and Nugget sat in my lap.

"You've got a chicken in your lap," Bernard or Perry said.

"I know," I growled.

"Never known anything like it," Uncle Brian said, putting a chunky sandwich in front of me. "That bird really has taken a shine to you."

Nugget began pecking at *my* sandwich.

"It's best not to make friends with the livestock," the other Bernard or Perry said. "They don't tend to stick around for long."

"Very true," Uncle Brian said, nodding.

Nugget gave me a questioning look.

"It's best you don't know what they're talking about," I whispered to him.

"Uncle Brian," I said as he pulled up a chair, "do you know what Earth's most valuable resource is?"

He rubbed his chin. "Cows, maybe?"

"Cows?" I said. Uncle Brian was clearly thinking about this from a very personal viewpoint.

"Yup," he replied. "Where would we be without milk? Or butter. Or burgers? Or cheese?"

I didn't know much about the Nurgles, but I didn't think that sending a cow up into space would show the best of what Earth has to offer. No offence to cows.

"I reckon manure is Earth's most valuable resource," Bernard or Perry said.

"Manure?" I said. I couldn't believe that was true.

"Think about it – it's nature's natural fertiliser. Without manure, there'd be no crops. Which would mean no food. Then we'd all be dead."

I couldn't argue with that, but there was no way I was going to send up a sack of animal poo to the Nurgles. They might take it as an insult. I didn't want to start an intergalactic war by mistake.

"What about tractors?" the other Bernard or Perry said. "Can't beat a good tractor."

Nugget covered his face with his wing and shook his head.

"You think Earth's most valuable resource is a tractor?" I said.

"No need to say it like that. Tractors are very important. Without tractors, we wouldn't be able to produce much food. And you know what that means."

"We'd all be dead?" I said.

Bernard or Perry nodded, his face serious.

"Does anyone have any ideas that aren't farm-based?" I asked.

All three of them looked at each other and shrugged.

Then Bernard or Perry said, "What about buckets?"

At that moment, I was a hundred per cent sure that Uncle Brian, Bernard and Perry were not going to find the answer to saving Earth.

"What's this for, Bertie?" Uncle Brian asked.

"A school project," I said quickly.

"You could always try searching on the internet," Uncle Brian said. "I've got a computer in the sitting room."

"Now that is a very good idea," I said.

CHAPTER 7

How do you find Earth's most valuable resource?

I don't think Uncle Brian uses his computer much because the keyboard was hidden under a stack of *Farmers Weekly* magazines.

"This is a computer?" Nugget said.

"Yup," I replied. "Computers can tell you the answer to anything."

"It looks very basic," Nugget said, and started pecking at the keys. "It's not doing anything."

"Just watch." I turned it on and typed our question into the search engine.

A surprising answer popped up.

"Data is the most valuable resource on Earth?" I read out loud.

"Amazing!" Nugget said. "I take back what I said about this computer being basic. Bring this data to me and I shall return to Nurgle-7 and Earth shall be saved."

"Brilliant!" I said. "That was easier than I thought it was going to be."

Nugget clapped his wings together. "Bring me the data, Bertie of Earth!" he said.

"OK!" I jumped up from my chair. "I'll bring you the data!"

I marched towards the door. Then stopped.

"What's the matter?" Nugget asked. "Is this data hard to find? Is it dangerous? What even is data? An animal, a fuel, a weapon?"

"Data is ..." I said.

"Data is what?" Nugget replied.

"Data is ... data."

"You don't know, do you?" Nugget said.

"I do not. Not exactly. But I can find out."

I sat back down and typed into the search engine again.

"Data is factual information that can be collected and studied to understand more about people and the world around us," I said.

"Data is information?" Nugget said. "How is that valuable? It doesn't sound valuable!" He grabbed my cheeks with his wings. "I am doomed! Earth is doomed!"

I felt a bit panicky. If data was the most valuable resource on Earth, I didn't really know what it was, or how I was going to collect it.

I typed in *Why is data valuable?*

"Data is timeless," I read. "It helps predict how people will behave."

"Why is that important?" Nugget said.

"I don't know!"

I typed again.

"It says if you have the right data, you can influence people," I read.

Nugget had a dark look in his already dark beady eyes. "So data allows you to control people," he said. "Interesting."

"What? Really?" I said. I had no idea how data could allow you to control people.

"I think the High Emperor would be very happy if I sent back some data," Nugget continued.

"I don't even know how you get data," I said, and pointed at the screen. "Look, it says oil is the second most valuable resource. I could get some of that. Uncle Brian is bound to have some in the kitchen."

Nugget slapped me round the face with his wing. Which didn't hurt because it was only made of feathers.

"The second most valuable resource!" Nugget said. "I can't take the High Emperor the *second* most valuable resource! Get me the data! Ask your computer where to find it!"

"Fine," I replied. "It says here you can buy data from companies who own it."

"Buy me the data then!" Nugget demanded.

"I'm a kid. I don't have any money!"

"Then the Earth is doomed! I am doomed!" Nugget jumped down and started running in circles. I thought about joining him.

"Wait!" I said, looking at the screen. "It also says you can collect your own data."

Nugget stopped running and cocked his head. "Collect it? How? With some kind of trap?"

"No, I can just find out information about people. Make our own data."

"What people?" Nugget asked.

"It will have to be Uncle Brian, I guess."

"You think information about your Uncle Brian is the most valuable resource on Earth?"

It didn't seem *that* likely, but what else did I have to go on?

"The computer says data is the most valuable resource," I said. "So, yeah, why not? Data is about people, and Uncle Brian might be a farmer, but he is still a person."

"I still don't understand how this data will give the Nurgles the power to control Earthlings," Nugget said.

"Hang on. You didn't say anything about the Nurgles controlling Earthlings."

Nugget shifted from foot to foot. "I didn't mean that," he said. "I meant I didn't understand why it is so important."

"Really?" I gave him my best glare, the one that Mum uses all the time when she wants me to tell the truth.

Nugget held up his wings. "I swear on my feathers."

CHAPTER 8

What's Oopsilon?

My plan to collect data was to follow Uncle Brian, note down interesting things about him and ask lots of questions. I wasn't sure what kind of data would be valuable, so I decided to just collect as much as I could.

"We can write all our data down in here," I said, grabbing a notepad from the table.

"Excellent," Nugget said. "What data shall we collect first?"

"Let's start with the basic stuff," I replied. "Name – Uncle Brian. Age – I'm not sure – old-ish. Shoe size …"

I went over and picked up one of his many wellies that were in a heap by the front door. "Size 13!" I said. "Impressive!" Then I looked at the label in a pair of his work dungarees which were hanging on a hook. "Oooh, XXL."

I looked around the house for more clues about Uncle Brian. There was a stack of fishing magazines on the table. "He enjoys fishing or at least likes looking at photographs of fish," I said, and wrote that down.

Nugget folded his wings. "Are you really sure that data is Earth's most valuable resource?"

"Is that the right attitude to save this planet?" I asked. "The internet said it was, so it has to be true."

Nugget shrugged. "Planet OO gave us Oopsilon."

"What's Oopsilon?" I asked.

"A substance that converts positive thoughts to energy."

That did sound pretty cool, but it didn't help me.

"Well, good for them," I said. "How about you start thinking positively and make yourself useful? Look around and see what you can find out about Uncle Brian."

Together, we found out what brand of toothpaste Uncle Brian uses, and that he washes his hair, body and face with the same bar of soap.

He must have had an achy back as he had a back massager. Probably from slinging haybales around all the time.

Uncle Brian also had a book by his bed that told him the meaning of dreams, so I made a note of that.

In the kitchen we found a bumper pack of lemon sherbets, so I wrote down that he was a fan of those.

"What are these golden orbs?" Nugget said, giving one a lick. "They are zingingly fabulous!"

He gobbled one down. I think it was too big for his throat because it got stuck. I was forced to do that thing where you have to squeeze someone's stomach to get the sweet to pop back out. Except I had to do it on an alien chicken.

And an egg popped out at the same time.

"Did that come out of me?" Nugget asked, his eyes a-goggle.

I picked the egg up off the floor and put it on the side. "I'll have that for my tea later!" I said.

Nugget squawked. "You're going to eat that egg? Knowing where it came from?"

I shrugged. "I'll just try not to think about that."

"Incredible," Nugget breathed.

"As we're done here, I reckon we should go out and grill Uncle Brian," I said.

"Why? Are you going to eat him too?"

"Grill as in question him," I explained. "You know, collect some more data."

We found Uncle Brian in the milking shed fixing one of the udder pumpers.

"That chicken's still with you!" he said. He looked back at the pump and shook his head. "Incredible."

"I am," Nugget said.

Uncle Brian looked up, surprised.

"I am very glad to be here," I said quickly, so he'd think it was me who'd spoken before.

Uncle Brian smiled and said, "I'm glad too." He sounded like he really meant it.

"Uncle Brian," I said. "I have a few questions for you."

"Is that so?"

"It's for my school project," I went on. "The internet said the world's most valuable resource is data, so I'm collecting some on you."

"Data, well I never! Fire away."

"Can you give me the most important data there is about you?" I asked.

Uncle Brian frowned.

I gave him a big smile. "Please?"

"Data ... I don't really know ... data."

"Anything you think that might be valuable to know about you," I continued.

Uncle Brian rubbed his hand over his stubble. "I don't think there is anything valuable to know about me."

"Well, what are you good at?" I said.

"I can sense when a cow is about to give birth."

"Wow, OK, I'll write that down. What else?"

"I've been told I make an excellent Victoria sponge," he said. "I'm pretty good at knitting too, truth be told."

"And what do you like doing in your spare time?"

"Farming," Uncle Brian replied.

"And?"

"Baking. Fishing. Knitting. Watching the TV."

"And what makes you happy?" I asked.

"Being with my nephew!"

I couldn't help but smile at that.

"And when I gut a fish and all the innards come out in one."

That wiped the smile off my face.

"And what are you scared of?"

"Scared, me?" Uncle Brian said. "Give over!"

"Everyone's scared of something," I replied.

"Not me."

"There must be something."

"There isn't," he insisted.

"There must be! What about an angry bull?"

"Nope."

"I can tell by your eyes there's something," I said.

"Loneliness. All right?" Uncle Brian said. "I'm scared of being lonely." He made a harrumph noise and turned back to his pump. "Now if you've got the data you need, I best be getting back to work."

CHAPTER 9

How can I send *that?*

I was pleased with all the data I had collected in such a short space of time, but Nugget wasn't so sure about it.

We went round to the back of the barn and sat on a haybale.

"I reckon we send this off to your Nurgle overlords and see what they think," I said.

Nugget flicked through the pages of the notepad with his beak. "You're sure about this?" he asked.

"Why don't we say it's just a sample?" I suggested. "See what they come back with? We can always get more data. Maybe from Bernard and Perry? The internet was very certain that data is the world's most valuable resource."

Nugget shrugged his feather shoulders. "Let's send it," he said.

I pulled his spacecraft out from where I'd hidden it in the haystack, and Nugget popped my notepad inside. Then he pressed a button with his beak. There was a crackling noise, followed by a bright flash of purple light.

"It's sent," Nugget said. "My Nurgle masters have beamed up your offering."

"What happens now?" I asked.

"They'll decide if what you've sent will save the world from total destruction."

"How long will that take?"

"About forty-five seconds," Nugget replied.

"WHAT?!"

"They'll either beam me back up, or there will be an explosion that will destroy the planet."

I looked up at the sky, very concerned that Uncle Brian's love of knitting and gutting fish might not be the things that would keep the Nurgles happy.

But then the spacecraft flashed again.

Nugget strutted over to it.

"They sent a message."

"What's it say?" I asked. "Are they going to blow up Earth?"

"Not yet."

"Not *yet*?"

"They're considering it," Nugget said. "The value of what you've sent isn't that clear. They would like you to send the following things to study."

"What things?"

"Loneliness, dreams and happiness."

"I can't send them those!" I said.

"Why not?"

"Because they're not actual things!"

"Well, Nurgles don't know what they are," Nugget said. "And what we don't know about interests us."

"But ... but ..."

"Let's start with loneliness. Where can we get some of that?"

"You don't *get* loneliness," I explained.

"Your uncle said it was what scared him. We are *very* interested in what scares people."

"But loneliness is a *feeling*, not a thing I can pop in a package and send into space."

"Then how can someone be afraid of it?" Nugget asked.

"I dunno really."

"What even is it?"

"When you feel like you're all on your own and that nobody cares about you," I said. "It's not nice to feel like that. I think that's why Uncle Brian is scared of being lonely."

"But there are 7.9 billion humans on Earth! How can anyone feel like they're on their own?"

"It's hard to explain."

"You don't need to explain it," Nugget said. "You need to get some loneliness so we can send it to the High Emperor. Then maybe us Nurgles can use it to scare our enemies and become master overlords of the universe!"

"Loneliness isn't a weapon!" I said. "It's just something that makes you feel like there's a hole inside you. Like something is missing."

"Like when your uncle pulls out the innards of a fish?"

"I suppose it does feel like that."

"You sound like you know this loneliness," Nugget said.

"When my dad left, I guess that's what I felt like."

"Left where?"

"Left home to live with his new family."

"But he still exists?" Nugget asked.

"Yes, he still exists."

"Then you can still speak to him? See him?"

"Yes," I replied.

"Then why are you lonely?"

"Because he has other people in his life now."

"Ah! So humans cannot share other humans or they get the loneliness?"

"No, we can share," I said. "It's just I don't feel like I'm as important. That Dad cares more about Nancy, that's my stepmum, and my new baby sister."

"Then you must exterminate this Nancy and the baby sister, and then your innards will feel better."

"No!" I said. "I don't want to exterminate them!"

Nugget cocked his head. "Then maybe they are not the source of your loneliness."

"Maybe I don't feel lonely at all," I said. "Maybe I feel ... jealous."

As I said it, I realised it was true. I suddenly felt like some of the hole that I had thought was in me had closed up.

"Thank you, Nugget," I said. "That chat really helped. Maybe I'm not lonely after all."

"Great. But making your innards feel better won't stop the planet being destroyed. You're going to need to send the High Emperor something, or pretty soon it will be KABOOM! Goodbye, Earth and all its cows and eggs and sherbet lemons!"

CHAPTER 10

What are dreams?

Nugget strutted about in front of me, his beady eyeballs locked on mine. "If you really can't send loneliness," he said, "can you send some of these dreams they've asked for?"

"Dreams aren't really a thing you can send," I said.

"Oh *really*? First loneliness, now dreams? The Emperor will think that you're being deceitful."

"It's true!" I said.

"So what are dreams? Explain."

"Dreams are two different things really."

"Two different things?" Nugget asked.

"They can be like stories that happen in your mind when you're asleep. They can be amazing or terrifying. They're often a bit strange and confusing."

"Terrifying is good. Send the Emperor some terrifying dreams."

"It doesn't work like that," I explained. "Dreams aren't something you can catch hold of. They just happen."

"So humans make up things in their heads?"

"Yes! But you don't have any control over them."

"How can that be?" Nugget asked. "If it is you that has created them?"

"I don't know really. They just happen to you when you sleep."

"But it is you that's making them happen! Why can't you control that?"

"I guess you can't control everything," I said.

"You can, if you have all of the most valuable resources in the universe."

"I don't think anything can control dreams. They're kind of untouchable."

"Untouchable?" Nugget said, tilting his head this way and that, as if he didn't understand.

"I guess there's lots on Earth that is untouchable," I continued. "I think dreams can show us what we want. Also what we are worried about."

"So data about dreams could be powerful? If you knew a person's dreams, you would know how to scare them. You'd know what to offer them to get them to do what you want?"

"I guess ... I'd never thought of it like that."

"I like the sound of dreams," Nugget said. "Are you sure you can't squeeze them out of someone's head? With an udder pumper maybe? Then we can send the dreams to the High Emperor?"

"No. You can't milk someone's dreams out of them."

Nugget looked disappointed. Then he cocked his head again. "Aha!" he cried. "You said dreams are two things. What else are they?"

"Dreams are also a person's biggest hopes and wishes."

"Hopes and wishes? Can we send those up to the Emperor?"

"Not really," I said. "They're not really things either. They're more feelings."

"Seriously? *Again?* How can Earth be so full of so many non-things and so many feely-things?"

"A dream, I suppose, is what someone wants in the future. A goal."

"Like the Nurgles want to be masters of the universe?" Nugget asked.

"Yes, exactly that! But I'm not sure the rest of the universe would be happy about that."

"Happiness! That is the third thing the Emperor wants!" Nugget said.

"I think it's something everyone wants," I said.

"Do not tell me we can't send some of that up to space."

I pulled a face. "Errr, not really."

Nugget sighed and said, "So tell me, what is this happiness?"

"Happiness is the warm glow you get inside when life feels good. Happiness is when your worries drift away. It's when you're around people that you love. And you just feel ... content."

Nugget shook his head. "Then it sounds like it is bye-bye, Earth!"

CHAPTER 11

So who are Nurgles really?

There had to be something I could do. But how could I send loneliness or dreams or even happiness to the Nurgles? It wasn't possible.

I paced around the yard, trying to think, with Nugget trotting along by my feet.

Suddenly, I came to a stop.

"Data," I said. "That's it!"

"What's it?" Nugget asked.

"If data can be used to control people and how they behave, then maybe I just need to collect some data about the Nurgles."

"Data about us?"

"Yes!" I said. "Don't you see? If I know more about you, maybe I will know what you are really after!"

"We are after becoming masters of the universe! That is our dream."

"But what makes you want to do that?"

"Isn't that obvious?" Nugget said. "So we are the most feared species in all the galaxies!"

"But why do you want to be feared?"

Nugget looked at me and didn't say anything at first. "I guess so we are not attacked," he finally replied.

"So you want to be feared because you're afraid?"

"The Nurgles are never afraid!" Nugget squawked. "Even when we were almost exterminated by the Keplorians, we were not scared. We were brave!"

"The Nurgles were almost exterminated? Sorry to hear that."

"But now no one attacks us! We attack them!"

"How many planets have you destroyed?" I asked.

Nugget scratched at the ground with his foot. "None. So far."

"None?"

"We haven't needed to destroy any. They've all sent their most valuable resource. Until now."

"I don't think the Nurgles really want to destroy planets!" I said.

"We do! We really, really do!"

"I think you're just trying to scare the other planets into believing you can destroy them so they don't attack you!" I said, and picked up my notepad. "Time to find out more about you Nurgles. How many of you are there?"

"There are three hundred and twenty."

I looked up. "Is that all?"

"We may be few, but we are mighty!" Nugget said.

"What weapons would you use to destroy planets?"

"Really powerful ones."

"Such as?" I asked.

"Lasers and explosives and sonic pulsing booms – that sort of thing."

"Hmm," I hmmed. "And what do you look like when you're not a chicken?"

"Fierce and scary."

"I'm going to need more than that."

"We have muscular shiny black bodies and powerful limbs," Nugget said.

"How many limbs?"

"Six."

"What else?" I asked.

"We stand at five thousand microns tall."

"Five thousand microns?" That sounded big, but hang on ... "Isn't a micron less than a millimetre?"

Nugget ignored that question and said, "We are very fierce and extremely scary!"

"Why are you chicken-sized now?" I asked.

"I told you, I transformed to blend in."

I put my pen down. "No offence, Nugget, but from what I'm hearing, I don't think the Nurgles are much of a threat. To be honest, from what you've said, you sound a bit like alien ants."

"We are very fierce and scary, OK?" Nugget insisted.

"Hmm," I hmmed again.

CHAPTER 12

What really is Earth's most valuable resource?

I sat down on the haybale while Nugget flapped about in a right old panic. He was trying very hard to convince me that the Earth really was under threat from the Nurgles.

I let Nugget get out what he wanted to say. Finally, he ran out of steam from all the flapping, and I put my hand on his head. "Listen, I have an idea," I said.

To be honest, I hadn't really believed the internet saying that data was the Earth's most valuable resource. But I was beginning to understand the power of data now. How it could be used for bad. But also for good.

"Nugget," I said. "I am going to give the Nurgles Earth's most valuable resource."

"You are?"

"See, I think we fear what we don't know."

"How do you mean?" Nugget asked.

"I was scared of the Nurgles because I didn't know anything about them."

"You are scared of the Nurgles because we are fierce and scary."

"Errr, OK," I said. "But I think the Nurgles are scared because they don't know anything about Earth. Maybe if you knew more about us, then you wouldn't fear us."

"The Nurgles fear nothing and no one!" Nugget said.

"Nugget, I think you're going to have to let that go. No one here is convinced."

He sank down so his legs disappeared under him. "Fine."

"I think the Earth's most valuable resource is friendship," I said.

"Friendship?"

"Yeah, friendship is what happens when you get to know somebody, learn about them and like them. Just like I've done with you."

"You like me?" Nugget asked.

"I do." I grinned. "Mum said I should make friends with the livestock. Seems I have."

"Something is happening!" Nugget said, rising to his feet. "I feel all warm and fizzy inside!"

"That's happiness," I said.

"I like the feel of it!"

"Good!" I laughed. "Me too! I want to send the Nurgles a friendship agreement," I said.

Nugget blinked. "Nice. But is it as good as Oopsilon?" he asked.

"Yes ... possibly! The internet may say that data is the world's most important resource," I said, "but I think it's what you do with data that really matters. I think what you learn about people should be used for good. To find ways to make connections. To help make friends."

I scribbled on my notepad and ripped out the page. "Here, send this up to the High Emperor."

Nugget read it out loud. "Bertie from Earth would like to extend an offer of friendship between Humans and the Nurgles. We would like to get to know you better, and for you to know us. We would like to share data for good. (P.S. I know you can't actually blow up the planet.)"

CHAPTER 13

What did I tell you about making friends with the livestock?

Seconds after we sent up my note, the spacecraft flashed purple, and Nugget stuck his head inside.

"So what did they say?" I asked.

"They accept the invitation!" Nugget replied. "Your planet has been saved! My mission is complete!"

"They were never going to blow Earth up, Nugget," I reminded him. "Not with your teeny tiny weapons."

"Just let me enjoy this moment," he said.

"So what now?" I asked.

"We must confirm it with the Nurgle agreement ritual!"

"Really?"

"Yes," Nugget said seriously. "The safety of your world depends on it."

I knew that wasn't true, but I banged my backside into his anyway.

Nugget pointed his wings to the sky. "Now, behold the arrival of the mighty Nurgles!"

"What? They're coming here? Now?" I said.

"You invited them!"

"I ... I ... didn't think ..." I looked up and saw five egg-shaped aircraft plummeting down from the sky over Long Bottom Farm.

Nugget lowered his head and said, "Bow down to those that are powerful, those that are strong, those that—"

"—are about to land in the cow field!" I interrupted. "Quick!"

We raced out of the yard and down the track to the cows. We were just in time to see the spacecraft land right in the middle of Uncle Brian's best milkers.

The little portholes on the spacecraft opened just as I was about to climb over the gate. I didn't see what stepped out because the Nurgles were so tiny.

Suddenly there was a purple flash, which was so bright I had to shut my eyes. When I opened them again, there were about twelve more cows than there had been before.

One of the cows stepped forward and said, "My name is Nooglynogglynoonoo, and

I am the High Emperor of Nurgle-7. Which of you is Bertie of Earth? Show yourself, friend! Greetings, Oh Great One!"

I did not mind being called Oh Great One, but I did feel a bit awkward about them thinking I was so important.

I jumped down off the gate and coughed. "Errr, I'm Bertie."

The High Emperor looked from me to the cows, then back to me. "Oh. I thought that those were humans."

"Nope, those are cows. Easy mistake to make," I said, to be kind. Clearly the Nurgles had *not* paid that much attention to the data I had sent them. Just shows you, data is only valuable if you bother to look at it carefully.

"We are here to collect Nugget," the High Emperor continued, "and to perform the Nurgle agreement ritual to bond our friendship."

"I've already done that!" I said quickly.

"But not with me, the High Emperor!"

So, yeah, I rubbed bums with an alien cow too.

Bernard or Perry just happened to be passing at the time. He shouted over the fence, "What did I tell you about making friends with the livestock?" Then shook his head and carried on.

"You must visit Nurgle-7," the High Emperor told me.

"*Really*? I could do that?" I said.

"Friends must stay in touch," the High Emperor said. "But for now, Nugget has to return with us."

"Oh," I said. Suddenly I felt a big wobble in my belly.

Nugget saluted the High Emperor, and they nodded back because I think cows might not be able to salute without falling over. Then there was another bright flash, and the cows were gone. Seconds later, the five spacecraft rose up from the ground and shot off into the sky.

Nugget then turned and saluted me. "Thank you, Bertie of Earth. I must now go. But I'll come and pick you up another time."

"I'd like that."

"When would suit you?"

"Same time next year?" I said, and Nugget nodded.

I walked Nugget back to his spacecraft, feeling a bit sad but also happy.

"I'll miss you," I said.

"I shall miss you too," Nugget replied.

I took a sherbet lemon from my pocket and put it in his spacecraft. "For the journey."

Nugget got back into his little egg capsule, waved goodbye and the door shut. It flashed bright purple, then shrank down to the size of a small pebble. The capsule whizzed off into the sky, making a sound like an angry bee.

I watched it go, and once it was out of sight I turned round. Uncle Brian was walking towards me.

"Where's that chicken you've bonded with?" he said.

"He's around," I replied, and looked upwards. "Somewhere."

"Look," Uncle Brian said, "I'm going to bring the cows in. I wondered if you might like to help. I promise no jokes this time."

"I'd like that," I said.

Uncle Brian smiled.

"I'm sorry I was grumpy when I got here," I added.

Uncle Brian ruffled my hair. "That's OK, kid. I understand."

"It's just we don't see each other often, and I don't really know you. But I'd like to hang out and get to know you more."

"I'd like that too," Uncle Brian said. "Hey, we could go fishing! I could show you how to gut one!"

"We could … or maybe you could show me how to bake a Victoria sponge instead."

"Whatever you like, kid."

"I like it here, Uncle Brian," I said. "And I think I'd like to come back *every* holiday."

"I didn't expect you to say that!" Uncle Brian said. "But I *am* pleased!"

I hadn't expected it either. But then I'd thought that I'd only find cows, pigs and sheep at Long Bottom Farm. Instead, I'd found a new friend and an invitation to another planet!

Now *that's* what I call an awesome summer holiday! I think my next one is going to be out of this world!

Our books are tested
for children and young people by
children and young people.

Thanks to everyone who consulted on
a manuscript for their time and effort in
helping us to make our books better
for our readers.